MY AMERICA

Freedom's Wings

Corey's Diary

by Sharon Dennis Wyeth

Scholastic Inc. New York

Kentucky
1857

August 9, 1857

Corey

Angel

Roland

Angel is Mama. Roland is Daddy. I be Corey. Age nine years old. My daddy made this book for me.

But my book must be a secrit. Do not let the Hart fambly see.

August 10, 1857

Daddy and I go to the woods. Our best thing be burds. Plenty of burds in these parts.

We listen to them sing. Sometimes we listen before sunrise.

This morning Daddy teaches me the whip-poor-will song. Daddy whistles and I whistle back. Then we work.

Mama found me a hidey hole for my book. A hidey hole in the oak tree.

August 11, 1857

My friends.

Mingo.

Mingo lives with Aunt Queen. Mingo is bigger than me. Mingo does not know his age. And Aunt Queen cannot recollect it.

Young Bob.

Young Bob can do what he pleases. He is the Hart fambly son. His father, Masser Bob Hart. His mother, Missus Susie.

Charles.

Daddy's friend. Charles sleeps in the shed.

Mingo and Charles and I pick tobacco. Young Bob plays with his marbles.

August 12, 1857

My daddy is a blacksmith. Today he went to Lexington. Before he went, Daddy and me watched burds.

Snow geese, flying high in the sky.

Today they are heading south say Daddy. In spring they will head north.

Lexington is in the south. I can spell the name, but I have not gone there.

North is where Mr. Frederick Douglass is. We have his newspaper hid 'neath the floor. The newspaper be called the *North Star*.

I can also spell Kentucky.

August 13, 1857

Too tired. Picking in the heat. All day long.

When snow geese fly, they do not make as much noise as some other geese do. Different kinds of geese at day. At night different kinds of owls.

August 14, 1857

Daddy still in Lexington. I writ in my book. Daddy say writ every day, son. Writ your mind.

Mama cannot writ. She cannot read. She say she scared to try. The owners don't like our people to writ and read.

Mama makes one hundred biscuits for the big house every morning.

Mama sews. Missus Susie say Mama sews even better than Aunt Queen. Mama also works the garden.

August 15, 1857

Red burd near my hidey hole. His song sounds like "pur-ty, pur-ty." I try to whistle the red burd's song. But I cannot. Get Daddy to teach me. I call him red burd, but his name be carrdnul.

Same Day, Later On

Today I writ two times in my book. Before my book, I writ in the dirt. In the dirt with a pointy stick. My daddy taught me in secrit.

August 16, 1857

Evening times, Aunt Queen and Mama make a quilt from scraps of cloth. Aunt Queen is Mingo's mother now. Mingo's real mother be sold farther south. Mingo cried when that happened. Masser Hart did that to Mingo's mother.

August 17, 1857

Mama is canning peaches in the big house. Missus Susie is canning, too. Aunt Queen is cuttin' up the pears for to make the jelly. Missus Susie calls me. She say, you fetch the water, Corey. Put it in the kettle. Then we will bile the jars.

Missus Susie say she will teach me to wait on the table. Her cuzins are coming to visit. Missus Susie say Mama must sew her some new red curtains. Sew some new red curtains for the parler. Missus say Masser Hart will buy the red cloth. Aunt Queen say to Mama that the Harts be puttin' on airs for that cuzin visit.

August 18, 1857

Daddy is home. He did some smith work in Lexington. Made right smart wages. But Masser Hart let him keep only a little bit. I hear Mama say that someday Daddy can make plenty of wages to buy our freedom. But Daddy say it will never happen. He could not make enough wages for that. Hard as Daddy works, Masser Hart takes almost every penney. That makes me angry.

Crows in the cornfield. Masser Hart tells me to chase them away. But when he is not lookin' I let the crows eat the corn. "Caw caw."

August 19, 1857

Daddy read my book. Say he is so proud of me. I am a double head. I read and I writ, also. Mama is proud. Keep both of them things in your double head, Corey, she say. Reading and writing. But do not let on that you know how. Masser Hart would not like that.

Daddy and I read our newspaper that is hid 'neath the floor. The *North Star*. Mr. Douglass wrote it. Mr. Douglass ran away and took his freedom.

The massers own our body. But our mind belongs to ourselves. That is what Daddy say.

Daddy gave me a spelling list to learn.

COUSIN
FAMILY
PARLOR
BOIL
BIRD
SECRET
PENNY
WRITE
CARDNUL (we are not certain about this one)

August 20, 1857

I try to sing like the red bird, but I can't. Daddy teaches me. The red bird whistles "pur-ty, pur-ty," say Daddy. I try, but I still cannot. When Daddy teaches me the robin's song, I do that fine.

"Cheer up, cheer up," sings the robin.

Same Day, Later On

Daddy worked at his forg. He made shoes for the horses. Young Bob let me ride his pony. Mingo was bringing in oats.

Young Bob say Mingo and me can play marbles with him. I won me a blue one off Young Bob. He let me keep it.

August 21, 1857

We go to church with the Hart family. Mama sewed the tears in my shirt. My shoes so big that I stumble.

We sit in the back with our people.

Young Bob sits with his family in the front.

A red-tailed hawk high in the sky, on the way home.

The Hart family leaves us be after church. And that is good.

Same Day, Later On

Aunt Queen makes ash cakes. She rolls cornpone in the cabbage leaves. Mingo and I help her. Mingo and I bury the cabbage leaves in the ashes of the fire. That way the ash cakes cook.

After we eat, Charles plays his banjo.

Mingo and I make hoops from the grapevines. I play with my blue marble. Daddy smokes a pipe.

Old screech owl makes a whinny. I make a whinny back at him. Aunt Queen laughs. She say I sound like that old screech owl, sure 'nuff. I might turn into a bird myself.

Mama sings, "Swing low, sweet cha-ri-ot." Her voice is sweeter than any bird.

August 22, 1857

Lot of corn comin' in. No time to rest. At supper, Missus Susie has me wait on the table. I got to learn how good, before the Hart cousins come. Hart family eats chicken. Smells too good. Our family has no chicken to eat. I am lookin' at that chicken and I drop a spoon. Missus slaps me hard 'cross the side of my head. Makes my ear start to ring.

Mama put a warm cloth on my ear. Daddy is angry.

August 23, 1857

Daddy showed me a warbler in the brush. That warbler hides good. Stays so still, it is hard to see him.

Sometimes I wish no one could see me. Then I would not be hit for droppin' the spoon.

Same Day, Later On

Missus Susie keeps Mama sewin' in the big house. The rest of us pick corn.

Mingo got an ache in his stomick. But he must still work. Charles puts Mingo in the shade and does his picking for him.

That Night

I went to my hidey hole to take out my marble. Mingo saw me. He saw my book.

I truss Mingo.

August 24, 1857

I work Mama's garden while she is at the big house. Pole beans and yams comin' in. When he comes from the forg, Daddy and I roast yams and put beans in a kettle. Charles comes by. Make somethin' to eat for us all.

August 25, 1857

Daddy read my book. He say I write almost as good as Frederick Douglass.

The bobwhite song sounds like its name.

Daddy say I might call a bobwhite to me if I get that song just right.

Daddy's Spelling List
TRUST
STOMACH
FORGE

August 26, 1857

Aunt Queen hurd that a traveling preacher is coming. The preacher is a free colored man. Daddy will ask Masser Hart if we can see that preacher when he comes. I have never seen a preacher the color of myself.

Same Day, Later On

Mama has made all the new red curtains. Missus Susie say she is pleased. Masser Hart will allow us to go hear the black preacher.

Mama is singing in the cornfield. "His eye is on the sparrow, so I know he's watching me."

Poor Mingo is sad. His own mama used to sing that song. Mingo thinks of his mama who got sold.

August 27, 1857

Bad news. Young Bob catch me at my hidey hole. He see the book. Say what do I need with a book, 'cause I cannot write or read? I beg him to say nothin'. He say my daddy better not be teaching me. His father tole Daddy he better not teach nobody to write and read, just because he does. I am scared.

Later On

I give Young Bob his blue marble back. Then he promises that he will not tell.

Woodpecker made a hole in a dead tree. New place to hide my book. Pray to God that Masser Young Bob keeps his promise. Else Masser Hart will take away my book. Worse, Daddy might get in trouble.

August 28, 1857

That freeman preacher was the best man that I have ever seen. He speaks grand. He also sings in a loud voice. Loud as the thunder. Mama sang with him, "I look over Jordan and what do I see? A band of angels coming after me."

Aunt Queen was crying. She said that preacher made her see the promised land.

Charles and Daddy talked with the preacher, when he was done preaching.

Same Day, Later On

Mingo and I played with our hoops. Young Bob played with us. Young Bob has said nothin' else about seeing my book. Could be that he forgot.

Later On, Evening

Daddy and I hear a sparrow song. The sparrow sings, "Oh, sweet Canada, Canada." Daddy say, someday we will go to Canada also. But be quiet 'bout that, Corey.

August 29, 1857

Missus Susie teaches me to wait on the table again. At the start, I do fine. But then I broke a teacup. The cup slipped out of my hand. She hit me with her iron key. Now I got a cut 'neath my eye.

Masser hit Mingo 'cross the back with a log. He caught Mingo eating his peaches. Young Bob watched his father hit Mingo with that log. Young Bob hung his head down when he saw that.

Daddy and I hear the bluebird singing in the orchard. Daddy say it troubles him that Missus hit me with her key and he can't stop her. It troubles him that Mingo got hit with that log. Daddy say when trouble is on his mind, the sweet bluebird song helps his mind to rest.

August 30, 1857

Preacher man came to our cabin at night. I was 'neath the table. I listened to all of them talkin'. I wake up in the morning to recollect it.

Talkin' about the Underground Railroad. It's not a train, but people who can help us.

Must cross the Ohio River. Ohio is a free state. More people there are free, so they will help us take our freedom, too.

White people also part of it. They will help us, too.

Charles don't trust that. Charles say he has not met the white person who will help him. Preacher man say, it is the truth. See a white man grab his ear and then look you in the eye straight, you can trust him. That is a signal for the Underground Railroad.

Later On

I hear Daddy speak up and say we gon' to run for it. Mama say, no. She is too scared.

I will keep my book hid 'neath the floor. So when I run north, my book will be near. I will take my book with me and write of my journey with the Underground Railroad.

September 1, 1857

We stood out in the dark, looking at the sky. Follow the drinkin' gourd, Daddy say. Remember. That is what the preacher man tole us.

Aunt Queen ain't goin' nowhere, she say. And she gon' keep Mingo with her. Charles say he is surely gon' to try.

What if we lose each other in the dark? Mama asks.

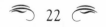

The whip-poor-will song, Daddy say. The whip-poor-will song will be our signal. The whip-poor-will sings in the dark.

September 2, 1857, Morning

I try to teach Mama the whip-poor-will song. But she cannot learn. Are we gon' run north? I ask her.

Get that thought out of your head, son, she tell me. If we get caught runnin', Masser might beat us or sell us.

That makes me scared.

Same Day, Later On

Mama made me a new red shirt! No more talk of running away.

September 3, 1857

Corn shuckin' festival. All day we shuck the corn. Then we have a party. That is the first time I wore my new red shirt. Never had a shirt so soft.

Aunt Queen made peach cobbler. Charles played his banjo. Mama sang.

Mingo and I played with our hoops.

Aunt Queen asked Daddy for some bird songs. Daddy say, ask my son. He is right smart at bird songs himself.

So I do the robin, the bobwhite, the whip-poor-will. I do the sparrow who sings oh, sweet Canada, Canada. Then I whinny like the screech owl. I leave out the red bird song, and throw in a duck call. Then I honk like a goose.

Aunt Queen laughed plenty at that goose.

She gave me a new name. Corey Birdsong. I like that.

Corey Birdsong. My new name.

September 4, 1857

Hart cousins came for the visit. I wait on the table. When I go to get more biscuits, I hurd them talkin'. I hear something so bad.

Masser Hart say he gon' sell Daddy. Gon' sell Daddy to one of his cousins.

Masser Hart say he will need a high price for a blacksmith good as Daddy. His cousin say he is willing to pay very high for that kind of worker. Take my breath away to hear those things.

They don't know I hurd them. I ran to tell Mama, then run back quick to the big house. Mama say she will go find Daddy at his forge.

Now Daddy is nowhere.

September 5, 1857

Hounds. I hear them barking. Mean dogs are after my daddy. Mama is crying. Run, Daddy, run.

Masser Hart hurt Mama's arm. Say, you stay put.

Daddy ran away with Charles. Left Mama and me behind.

September 6, 1857

Masser Hart rode out on his horse. He has gone to look for Daddy. He took many men with him. He took his cousin with him, also.

Mama say Daddy was sad to leave us. But she told him to run as fast as he could. We would only hold him back, Mama say. Make him go slower. She did not want Daddy sold.

We pray for Daddy and Charles.

September 7, 1857

Still no word about Daddy and Charles. Masser Hart has not come back. I wait on the table in the big house. Missus is cross with me. Some of the cousins are still here. Stay out of their way, warns Aunt Queen.

My heart feels sick, when I think of those men and dogs after Daddy and Charles. What will happen, if they are caught?

Does Daddy have food? Mama say he and Charles took a sack with them. Sack full of corn.

Run, Daddy, run.

September 8, 1857

Mingo say not to be sad. If Daddy was sold to the Hart cousins, it would be worse. Hart cousins live in the Deep South. I would never see Daddy anymore in my life. Now Daddy will be free. I will see him again someday.

September 9, 1857

I hurd Mama cry last night.

Today Aunt Queen was singing in the yard, "Steal away, steal away home." Missus shout at Aunt Queen to be quiet.

Tonight Mama goes to the cornfield and stands there still as can be. She is thinking of Daddy.

September 10, 1857

Before sunset, Mingo and I get kindling in the woods. Everything is so quiet. Then we see an owl with long ears. He was sitting in a tree.

That owl looked right at me. Then he sang, "Hoo, hoo," like he is trying to tell me

something. Might be that owl has seen Daddy and Charles, I tell Mingo.

Mingo say I put too much store by the birds. Birds don't know much of anything.

I think birds know plenty. Some fly north to south and back again. They see the whole world and all us people. An owl does not sleep at night. That is when he flies.

Big storm heading this way.

September 11, 1857

Charles is caught.

September 12, 1857

Masser Hart and his cousin brought Charles home. Then they beat Charles in the yard. Charles beat so bad he cannot stand up afterward.

Aunt Queen crying. Mama praying. Mingo and I so scared. Think that beating might kill Charles.

Young Bob saw everything. When he saw, Young Bob ran off to the stable. I think Young Bob wants nothin' to do with it.

Please, God. Do not let them catch my daddy and beat him, too.

September 15, 1857

I have not written for a spell. Mama told me not to. The Hart cousins are gone. But Masser Hart was watching us all the time. He is so angry that Daddy was not caught. Mama is afraid that he will catch me with my book. Then he will beat me like he beat Charles. But today Masser Hart went to Lexington.

I am hiding in the place back of the shed. Everything is quiet. Just hear the crows.

Charles is working again. Aunt Queen put herbs on his back to draw out the pison.

But where is Daddy?

September 16, 1857

Charles tole us about what happened with Daddy and him.

They were hiding alongside a creek. Big storm came and they got lost. Lost each other in that storm. Couldn't see for the rain. Couldn't hear for the thunder.

Next thing Charles knows, he is caught. Masser Hart is there. Tied him up. Dogs biting at him.

Didn't catch Daddy, though.

Charles say Daddy runs faster than any man or dog. Could be that he will make it 'cross the Ohio River.

Mama and I pray that it is so.

September 17, 1857

Masser Hart came home. Young Bob came to the field with a poster. I let on to Young Bob that I can't read it. But he leave it lay at my feet, anyway.

REWARD — ONE HUNDRED DOLLARS.

RUNAWAY SLAVE, NAME OF ROLAND.

FINE BLACKSMITH. READS AND WRITES.

SMART TALKER. TALL AND GOOD-LOOKING.

That is Daddy the poster is talkin' about.

Aunt Queen say she hurd that the slave catchers are thick as flies in Lexington. They want to make the money from the reward.

September 20, 1857

Missus got me working her garden. Digging 'taters and picking okra. Got me bringing in the melons.

Nighttime comes and I work our own garden at home. Mama gives me supper. Tonight we had corn bread and pot likker.

Now I must go to the stable to care for the horses.

Same Day, Later On

Missus hurd me in the yard. She hurd me call the bobwhite. She hurd me sing to the robin. I did not know that Missus was listening. Missus say you know plenty 'bout birds, don't you Corey? I tell her that I know a few things.

But I do not tell her that my name is Corey Birdsong. My new name is for myself. It is not for the Hart family.

October 5, 1857

Every morning I go to the woods. Sometimes I run clear to the creek. There I sing the whip-poor-will song. But Daddy never answers. I thought that he might come back for us. Leastwise, he is free and that is so good.

I do not feel like writing in my book. With Daddy gone, there is no one to read it. Besides, my mind is empty. The one and only thought I have is how I miss my daddy, Roland.

November 1, 1857

Masser Hart offers one hundred and fifty dollars reward for Daddy. Charles hurd this in the stable and tole us.

November 15, 1857

Masser took me to Lexington to haul the oats for him. Young Bob went along, also. Big place with plenty of people. Bad happenings, however. A man was chained to a post in a wagon. It is cold, but he had no shirt on him. I do think it was the freeman preacher. My heart is so sad to see that. Young Bob say he think the preacher is in trouble, 'cause he help the runaways. I close my eyes when we drive back. Do not want to see nothin' after that.

November 30, 1857

Mingo asks me about my book. I tell him I forget about that book. I do not want to write anymore. He say he wants to learn to write his name. He asks me to teach him.

So I teach him his letters. First, he does not write in the book. We use the end of a burned stick. Scratch out the letters on a piece of wood.

Later

MINGO

He wrote this.

December 26, 1857

Almost a month since I took out my book. But I want to try my Christmus gif' from Mama. It is a red feather quill for writing. Mama made it for me. She say, keep writing, Corey. Do not forget how. But even if I could think of what to write about, I cannot write much. My ink is all run

January 5, 1858

A new bottle of ink. I went to my old hidey hole in the oak tree. Ink in there with Young Bob's blue marble. Young Bob did this. I think so. Can I trust him? I take the ink, but leave the marble.

Many birds are gone. But the owls are still here.

Where are you, Daddy?

January 15, 1858, Morning

Mama is feeling poorly. I do hope that Mama is not sick.

Same Day, Night

Mama say she knows that I am pining for my daddy. But I should let my mind rest from

that. Be happy that he is free. She tells me not to give up on my writing. She does not want me to lose my double head. Reading and writing are what Daddy wanted for me. The massers do not like it when you read and write, because reading and writing give you power. That is what Mama says. But what can I write? I ask her. My mind is empty. Mama say, write what you see. Someday, with God's help, your Daddy may read it. Write your book for him.

February 5, 1858

I see ice.

Mingo cuttin' ice on the creek.

I see Aunt Queen. Her back bent, because it is windy.

I see Charles tending the mule. The mule is sick. But Charles can fix him.

I see me hauling wood to the big house. Mingo and I make the fires.

Mama's footsteps in the snow. She makes corn bread for Missus. Mama is tired.

A bald eagle flying high. Sparrow with a white throat singing. He is spending the winter here, too.

Night comes, I see the sky. A star like ice, cut from the creek.

March 9, 1858

Masser called me to the house. A man from up north has come to buy horses. The man is named Mr. Renfield. But he also asks about birds. Birds be his best thing, it sounds like.

Missus tells him that I know a few things about the birds. I say that I will go with Mr. Renfield to show him some birds in these parts.

Mr. Renfield went outdoors with me and said thank you. He shook my hand. He shook my hand and he is a white man. Mingo says do not trust him.

March 10, 1858

Mr. Renfield took me in his buggy. He say he wants to see hawks. We stop near the field and I walk with him up the hill. Daddy and I saw hawks in that place once upon a time. Sure 'nuff, Mr. Renfield and I see hawks there. Red-tailed hawks flying with snakes in their mouths. The snakes are still sleepy from wintertime. So the hawks got them easy.

Mr. Renfield wants to take me in his buggy again.

March 11, 1858

Mr. Renfield asked to see a warbler he doesn't see too much in the north. The quiet kind who hides in the brush. I found one for him. They are hard to see. But they sing, "Tee-oh."

Then Mr. Renfield asks me if I know a sparrow who sings, "Oh, sweet Canada, Canada." I say I do. He looked me in the eye and grabbed his ear. Maybe he is from the Underground Railroad!

March 13, 1858

Yesterday Mr. Renfield was with Masser Hart all day. But this morning he came to find me. We went into the woods and saw a robin. Springtime is surely here. We listen to the robin sing. Can you sing the robin's song? Mr. Renfield asks me. I sing the song, "Cheer up, cheer up."

Then Mr. Renfield say, very good, Corey Birdsong.

I do not know what to think. Few folks know my new name.

Then Mr. Renfield say, I have seen your father Roland. I have come from the North to help you.

March 14, 1858

Mr. Renfield came to our cabin at night. He gave us news of Daddy. He is alive and still heading north.

Mr. Renfield met Daddy in Columbus, Ohio, at the home of a friend. Daddy's arm was hurt then. Slave catchers had cut him bad.

When Daddy gets farther north, he will try to find work. He is heading for a place by the name of Oberlin. He wants to come back for his family soon as he is able.

Mr. Renfield say Daddy's plan is not safe. Masser Hart's reward for Daddy is quite high. Many are out looking for him. Mr. Renfield thinks that Mama and I should run away on our own. Meet up with Daddy.

March 15, 1858

Mr. Renfield will take us north for a piece in his buggy. Then we must walk at night through the woods. In Kentucky, we will be on our own quite a bit. But Mr. Renfield has a friend we can meet up with. She is a schoolteacher.

When we cross the Ohio River, there are more conductors to help us on our way. Conductors on the Underground Railroad.

The wurds go through my mind like a stream. I am ready, I tell Mr. Renfield.

But Mama is quiet.

March 16, 1858

Mama does not want to go. She tole me that she is having a new baby. I did not know a thing about it.

Mama say that she will not be able to run fast.

I say that my new brother or sister should have freedom. I beg her.

Mama will think on it.

March 17, 1858

Snow geese fly north.

I show Mama.

I want to go where they are going.

Trust me, I tell her. This is our time.

I do trust, Mama tells me. But I am scared. Do not want my son hurt.

Let us take our chance, Mama. We must choose quick, while Mr. Renfield is here. I want to be free. I want to see Daddy.

Mama say, we will try. We will take this chance that God has sent us.

March 18, 1858

Mingo wants to run, too. But Aunt Queen will not let him. Charles will stay here with Mingo. I do not like to part with my friends.

March 19, 1858

Young Bob is sick. Aunt Queen must take care of him. Masser Hart and Missus Susie gone to Lexington. They took Charles.

Mr. Renfield say farewell to the Hart family and left, too. But he will return. Mama and I know.

March 21, 1858

Bread is in the sack. I will wrap my book up in my red shirt. We are waiting for Mr. Renfield. Lie flat in the buggy.

Gave Mingo my hoop. He is my brother. It pains me so to leave him behind.

March 22, 1858

Mama and me ran. Our turn to fly. We will meet up with Daddy someday. Mr. Renfield said we will make that happen.

Mama and me in a cave.

Got onions rubbed on our feet. Them dogs can't smell us that way. We wait for dark. No one can see us. Follow the drinkin' gourd, say Mr. Renfield. You will taste your freedom. What does freedom taste like? Where is Daddy?

The walls of the cave are covered with bats. The bats are sleeping.

March 23, 1858

Drinkin' gourd so clear last night. So bright I saw Mama's face in the dark. She was smiling. We must walk three nights and then head toward the road again. Slave catchers on the road. Be most careful.

Mr. Renfield's friend has her house just off that road. We must look out for a red door. When we reach that spot, we will have fifty more miles to the Ohio River. Mr. Renfield say he will send wurd to his friend, the schoolteacher. Tell her to listen out for a robin. Made us a hidey hole in the brush just like the warbler. Cover ourselves with tree branches.

March 24, 1858

Dogs barking. Hear them through the woods. How far back are they?

Keep rubbing our feet with onions. Walk in the creek water. Dogs can't smell us then. I hope.

Mama tripped on a root. Hurt her ankle.

March 25, 1858

Sky cloudy last night. We could not see the drinkin' gourd. I think we walked around in a circle. We hid out in a ditch close to the creek. Do not hear the dogs. Have we lost them? I hope so.

Plenty of owls in these parts. Saw the screech owl's yellow eyes. Owl made a whinny. I do not whinny. Must be quiet as we can be.

March 26, 1858

We were hiding in a ditch. A lady our color came upon us. We lie still. She said nothing. Only left a plate of stew on a rock. When she was gone, Mama and I ate. We were hungry. Our bread is all gone.

Where did the lady come from? Have we come to the road without knowing it?

Mama's ankle is swelled more.

March 27, 1858

Another cloudy night. We walked and walked, not knowing if we were heading north. In the morning, I saw snow geese flying. Now I know for sure. We are heading in the right direction. Found a field of high grass with blue flowers. So peaceful a place, but we are always afraid.

March 28, 1858

Last night the sky was clear. The drinkin' gourd was there to guide us. Mama's ankle is slowing her. She tries not to let on that it hurts her. I fear that we have gone past the red door. Mr. Renfield said the road is east. We head toward it.

Ate turtel eggs.

March 29, 1858

It was sunrise when we crept near the road. People were out in wagons. We laid flat in the brush, so as not to be seen. Then we had a scare. Loud gunfire.

Mama held me down when I tried to look at what was going on. Finally, I was up on my knees. The whole sky dark with passenger pigeons. Men with guns were lined up. Firing up into the air. Pigeons fell from the sky. Too tired to write now. More later.

Same Day, Later On

We creep out again, looking for the red door. I see a sign on the road. MAYSVILLE, 50 MILES. I can read the sign. Maysville is where the Ohio River is at, Mama say. We are at the spot that Mr. Renfield tole us about.

Then, through the trees, Mama spies the red door. But that house is across the road. Wagons are going up and down. We can not cross the road without being seen.

We laid still in the brush until evening. Then I began the robin song. That is the signal I tell Mama. Remember? After some time, a lady comes. She stands so close to us. But does not see us. I see her. I take a chance. I sing the robin song. She signals back. I stand up and so does Mama. We run with her to —

March 30, 1858

I fell asleep writing last night. It is another day. Mr. Renfield's friend is a teacher. Her name be Elsie. The house with the red door is a schoolhouse. Elsie brings us ham and corn bread to the cellar. There are tunnels dug in the wall, where Mama and I sleep.

Elsie puts herbs on Mama's ankle. Mama rests.

The new baby is still inside of her.

Upstairs I hear the voices of the children in the school. They are learning. I will go to school someday. I will. I will.

Same Day, Later On

Elsie showed me a spelling book!
I have a new spelling list.

GIFT
HEARD
WORD
POISON
TOLD

Same Day, Later On

Something quite bad happened. Masser
Hart himself came here. I heard his loud voice
upstairs. He say something, then he left. Mama
and I hid in our tunnels.

Later, Elsie came to show us a poster. A
poster about us.

RAN AWAY

A WOMAN NAME OF ANGEL AND HER BOY, COREY.

ANGEL IS GOOD SEAMSTRESS. SHE IS EXPECTING

A CHILD. THE BOY, COREY, IS NINE YEARS OLD.

HE IS WEARING A RED SHIRT.

REWARD TWO HUNDRED DOLLARS

FOR WOMAN AND BOY.

Elsie read the poster to us. But I could also read it myself. I will not be going back to the Harts.

March 31, 1858

Elsie is afraid for us to leave. But she say Masser Hart might come back, so we must leave. She will send word to a friend of hers that a robin and his mama are making their way north. Use the same signal, she tells me.

April 1, 1858

We began our journey again last night. Mama is so worried. The poster says she is expecting a child. People will know who she is at once, if they see her. Mama thinks we should go back to the Hart place. She say Masser Hart will not be so mean if we give ourselves up. I say I will not. The poster say I am wearing a red shirt. But my red shirt is in the sack.

April 2, 1858

Another clear night. Mama is in good spirits. Two barred owls were having a shouting match. Like to scared Mama to death. Mama laughed when I told her it was only two birds trying to out-hoot each other. Mama would rather be scared by a bird than by a man, anytime.

April 3, 1858

Followed a swarm of bats and found their cave. Good hiding place for us. Mama told me about her own mama and daddy. She never knew her mama. She died of the collarah when Mama was a baby. Showed Mama my book. She cannot read what I write. But I did teach her to read her own name. She can also read mine and Daddy's.

April 6, 1858

Rain all day. Rain all night. Bad dream that Masser Hart found us. Blisster on the heel of my foot.

April 7, 1858

Food all ate. Mama slower and slower. She cries. I wish I was an eagle. I could fly Mama on my back.

April 9, 1858

The moon was full last night. We went near the road. There was a house with nobody in it. I walked right up. Grabbed a chicken. Mama wrung its neck. We ran to the woods and made a fire. Ate that bird up. So hungry, couldn't be worried about the slave catchers.

April 10, 1858

Man with his cart in the middle of the woods. A man our color. Came right up on us in the brush. Like he was out looking for us.

He told us not to be scared. Gave Mama a ride in the cart. Walk in the water, he say. Dogs are out. You gettin' close to the Ohio River. But closer you get to freedom, the more slave catchers there are.

April 11, 1858

Walking. Creek so cold. Can't feel my feet hardly. Mama not that slow now. She pulls me along some. Says that my baby brother or sister is helping her feel stronger. Mama sings a song in a quiet voice, "Guide my feet while I run this race. Guide my feet while I run this race."

My insides shake. Mama say we must keep going.

Same Day, Later On

Caught a trout. We were half starving. How far is it to the Ohio River? I do not know.

April 13, 1858

We were crawling when she found us. She was an old woman picking mushrooms. She is a slave, too. Her name is Nerva. Nerva takes us to her barn through high grass. Her owners are away, she say. She tells us someone has been asking for us. Mama is scared. Did a Masser Hart come around here? Mama asks. No, another man was asking around about a boy and his mama, Nerva say. A colored man was asking that. Who is it? I wonder.

I help Mama get up to the barn loft. Night came. Nerva brought us mush. Tomorrow I will take you to a place, she tells us. You are not far from the river.

Barn swallow sleeping right next to us. There is light from the moon. So I write. I cannot stop myself from writing.

April 15, 1858

To tell what happened afterward. That next morning, Nerva took us back through high grass. Though she is old, she had us running. We came to a big hole at the foot of a hill. It was like a gopher house dug into the grass. Mama and I got in. She covered us over with branches. Nerva say, you wait here. Dark down there. But cool.

We stay for hours, it seems like. Cannot see the light, so we don't know what time of day it is. Then I hear someone moving around up there. I dare to sing the robin song. Mama hushes me. But I sing it another time, "Cheer up, cheer up."

Those branches move out of the way that minute. I see that now it is dark outside. A hand reaches down into the hole for us.

We hear a man's voice. "I am a friend. My name is John Parker."

To finish the tale.

I felt his hand. He took us to his boat. We got in and laid down flat. Oars splashed in the water. Boat rockin' from side to side. Going downstream, it felt like.

On the blackest night we made it over. We have crossed the Ohio River.

April 16, 1858
Ripley, Ohio

Home of Reverend Rankin. Part of the Underground Railroad, like John Parker who crossed us in his boat.

The house is on top a hill. We saw the light in the window when we got out of the boat. Walked up what seemed to be a hundred stairs to get here. John Parker helped Mama walk up those many stairs in the dark.

Then Mama and I slept in beds. Reverend Rankin say, we got to keep moving. Friends will take us on. Ohio is a free state, but we are runaways still. Slave catchers cross the river, too. The law lets them catch us if they can.

April 17, 1858
Red Oak, Ohio

Another night came. They led us out the back door. A wagon was waiting for us. No names of the people who helped us.

Now we hide in a church with thick walls. White folks and black folks givin' us food. Color don't matter here, it seems.

April 18, 1858
Gist, Ohio

Is this heaven where people my color have their own store just like the store I saw in Lexington? The people of Gist feed us food so fine! Lady fixed the blisster on my foot. Give Mama new clothes. Her old clothes are tore up and don't fit anymore.

Out the window, I spied a boy who looks something like me runnin' up and down the street like he is not scared of nobody in this world. My arms feel like wings, just to see him.

April 19, 1858
Sunday

In the town of Gist, they have a church with a colored preacher that does not travel around, but stays only in this place. What fine singing! Mama cried so. Cried for joy.

Everyone takes us in, like we are family.

Saw a flock of wild turkeys struttin' down the street.

Afraid that maybe we ate one for supper. There was a roast turkey on the table with so much other food. I have never seen food like that, even at the Hart table. We are at the home of a Mr. George Washington Lewis. He is a freeman. All the people in Gist are free.

April 20, 1858

I never do want to leave the town of Gist. But we must. Slave catchers raided the town this morning. Mrs. Lewis hid Mama and me in the attic. Mr. Lewis faced the catchers down. Stood with a gun at the front of his house. Dared those catchers to pass through his door. Catchers gave up and left. But Mama and I must go. No place is safe for very long.

April 21, 1858

Mr. Lewis saw me writing. Gave me more ink. This afternoon Mr. Lewis and his sons will ride with us to the next place. I will make my way to the next stop hidden in a coffin! I hope there will be air for me to breathe. Mr. Lewis say there are some small holes in the coffin.

Mama will sit in front of the wagon and wear a black hat and make sounds like she is crying. People on the road will think it is my funneral. Hope it will not be.

April 23, 1858

Rode in that coffin clear to Columbus. Passed through and did not see the city. I am worn out from being in that small space for such a long spell. Hard to stand. At night we rested on the side of the road. Mama passed food and water to me, which I ate inside the coffin.

April 25, 1858

Owl Creek. Had a bath. I smelled worse than a skunk.

Quaker people have taken us in. Mr. Lewis and his son have gone home to Gist. Mama is feeling poorly and cannot rise from her bed. Good soup. Kind people. We sleep in the stable in a far corner, so as not to be seen.

April 26, 1858

Mama sitting up in bed. Something else good as well. A trapper came through, name of Tut. He say he heard of Roland Birdsong! This Roland was on his way to Oberlin. That is the same place that Mr. Renfield said Daddy talked about. We will go to Oberlin soon as Mama feels rested.

April 27, 1858

One of the Quaker women say Mama cannot travel now. This woman knows about babies and such. Mama must stay with them until the baby is born. Else the baby might die. They will keep on hidin' Mama.

What am I to do? Daddy might be waiting for us. Or maybe he is going back south by this time to look for us. Mama say Daddy might have seen the poster about me and her. Then he knows we are on our way north as well.

April 28, 1858

Tut tells me that we are not so very far from Oberlin. If I find Daddy, we can come back for Mama and the new baby. Tut say he will help me find my father. I tell Mama I want to take this chance. Mama say go ahead son. I will not stop you. I feel I must keep going. But my heart is breaking.

Next night

Tut say he is tuff. He can wrastle a bear. Got the skin of a bear on his horse. Got plenty of hides from his trappin'. When I ride with Tut, I lie across his horse and he covers me with the hides. We go anyplace this way. People thought I was a dead man once. Now they think that I'm a bear. Cannot write in the day anymore, so I write by the fire. My writing has become my best thing to do.

Nighttimes, we head for the trees. Water the horse at the creek. Tut say if the catchers track us down, he wants me to run without him. Tut got his freedom papers. Freedom papers sewn in his shirt.

Two nights later

Today, we kept to the woods the whole time. I heard a bobwhite. I whistled the bobwhite song and the bird flew out of a thicket and came to me. I know a few things about birds, I tell Tut.

? 1858

I have lost track of time. Tut tells me stories. He tells me about Brother Fox and Brother Rabbit. He tells me how he ran away and took his freedom when he was only a boy. We travel both day and night and rest when we need to.

? 1858

Tut does not know the date either.

I ask Tut something that was on my mind.

Did my Daddy say that his name was Roland Birdsong, sure 'nuff? Birdsong is only my name, I tell Tut.

That is the name your daddy gave, Tut tells me. Roland Birdsong.

Daddy must have been thinking about me then.

I listen for the whip-poor-will. I hear one. But it is a bird this time. One day it will be Daddy. I recollect his signal. Can hear it in my mind.

Another Day

Clear sky last night. Made good time.

This morning Tut and I saw a marsh hawk. The bird was dippin' in the sky. Look like he was dancin'.

Same Day, Later

Tut taken. What to do?

Next Evening

Write it down.

I ran like he told me. I was at the creek when the catchers rode up out of nowhere. First I hid. They didn't see me. Tut showed them his freedom papers sewn in his shirt. Catchers tore those papers up. Tied Tut in ropes.

Took four men to drag him away. What will happen to my friend?

Later

Still heading north. Sky clear. Stars will be bright.

Another Day, 1858

Strayed from the creeks. Had no water to drink. Found a wood duck nest in the hole of a tree. Ducks nest close to water. Watched the ducks come over. Followed their path in the sky. Found a lake.

Another Day, 1858

Marshland. Skeeter bugs eatin' me alive. Bites on my arms and legs. Bleeding. Put mud on them. Green berries make me sick.

Later, 1858

Why do I write? Someday Daddy will read it. I am lost.

Another Day, 1858

So alone. I must be near Oberlin. But I see no road. Slept most of the day in a hidey hole 'neath a hollow log. When I wake, I hear a sparrow singing, "Oh, sweet Canada, Canada." The bird followed me here? Show me where, sparrow. Bird flew away.

Later, 1858

Stir crazy. Saw a red bird. Made myself sing the song over and over, "Pur-ty pur-ty." No one is anywhere to be seen. No path. No Angel, no Roland, no Tut.

Night

I see so well in the dark now, that I can even write. Thought of Young Bob. Saw his face at the window. He waved when we were leaving. Thought of Mingo. Will go back for him someday.

Another Day, 1858

How long has it been?

Screech owl makes a whinny first thing in the morning, last thing before dark. Keeps me going.

Bluebird sings, "Sleep and rest." Hiding in a canebrake. Found good berries.

Morning

I am lost. That's certain. But at night I see the star and head north. I am not as scared now. No sign of slave catchers or anyone else. During the day, I keep my mind at rest by listening to birds.

LARK
CHICKADEE
FEE-BEE
CARDNUL
JAY
BLUEBIRD
MOCKINGBIRD
OWL
ROBIN

I hear them all. Even when I cannot see them, they tell me they are with me.

Some days have passed.

Heat high.
Buzards circling.

May 20, 1858

For some weeks I was lost. I woke up in a graveyard. A crow stood next to my head. The undertaker found me.

May 21, 1858

He and his wife gave me food. I am no longer hungry. I have asked them to take me to Oberlin. They are conductors.

Thank you God. I am still alive and with the Underground Railroad again.

May 22, 1858

I was passed along again. This time my conductor was an Indian man. The undertaker and his wife asked him to ride me to where I wanted to go. I sat on the horse behind him, wearing Indian clothes.

I was half out of my mind some of the time I was alone. But I did not let go of my sack with my book and red shirt in it. My conductor's name is Thomas Fast Horse. A good name. Thomas also likes the name of Birdsong. I tell him how I got it. He can also sing like a whip-poor-will.

May 28, 1858
Oberlin, Ohio

Much has happened. I am staying with a student in Oberlin. His name is Dodd. He is my color and goes to college. I have never met anybody as smart as Dodd. I think he might be as smart as Mr. Douglass. Dodd also reads the *North Star*. He has books that belong only to himself. I have never owned a book, except the one I write in.

I have written a letter to Mama to let her know I am safe. Dodd knows a way to get my letter down to Owl Creek, where Mama is staying. The Quaker people will read the letter to her. I wonder about my baby brother or sister. If the baby is born yet.

May 29, 1858

Dodd has asked people he knows about Roland Birdsong. No one has seen him or heard of him. I do not know what to do next. Dodd say we will ask other people he knows at the meeting tonight. The meeting of abolishionists.

May 30, 1858
Late

My mind is on fire from the meeting.

The Underground Railroad is powerful. Many people do not believe in slavery. Many are willing to help people like me and my family find their way to freedom. I did not know until the meeting tonight that the law punishes people who help.

Dodd can go to jail for helping me. I am afraid for him. I remember what happened to my friend Tut. I was the cause of his trouble.

Dodd asked some friends at the meeting about Roland Birdsong. No news of him, however.

May 31, 1858

I want to go out looking for Daddy. Dodd say it is not safe. Even this far north, slave catchers take people back. They want the reward so badly.

A lady friend of Dodd's came to visit. Her name is Mary Ellen. She asked me to tell her my story. I told as much as I could recollect. She wrote down some of what I told her. Mary Ellen say the country needs to know how bad things are down in the South. We all must work to change that.

June 1, 1858

Still no word 'bout Daddy. I might give up hope. Could it be that he has gone south again to find us? Mary Ellen brought a poster today about Mama and me. Our reward is higher. If

Daddy was in Oberlin, he must have seen the poster. He must know we have run from the Harts. I am worried that Daddy got hurt by slave catchers or worse.

June 2, 1858

I asked Dodd today if he wants to read my book. He read it. You write well, Corey, he say. You are a brave person, all you have been through. I ask him about my spelling words.

Dodd's Spelling List
ABOLITIONISTS
PHOÉBE
CARDINAL
TOUGH
TURTLE
WRESTLE
FUNERAL

BUZZARDS
BLISTER
CHOLERA

Dodd say he did see that I spelled masser in the wrong manner, too. Masser is a word I do not want to spell the right way, I tell him. Masser is a word I do not ever want to spell again, matter of fact. Dodd laughs.

Then he say, do not let this book be seen by any strangers. You put some names of people who helped you in it. That could mean trouble for them.

I feel bad about that. I will burn this book before I allow it to trouble my friends any.

June 3, 1858

Mary Ellen and Dodd ask everywhere for Daddy. I need to go look for him myself. But

they make me stay in Dodd's room all the time. I am restless.

June 4, 1858

I am full of worry. Not only about Daddy, but about Mama. Dodd and Mary Ellen say I must not go back to Owl Creek though. Wait for Mama to make it up here they say. Then Mama and I can go to Canada and be free forever. I cry when I hear them say that. I think they have given up hope of finding Daddy.

I stand by the window all the time, whistling the whip-poor-will's song. Don't care what folks think. Don't care who sees me.

Please help me God. I just can't sit here and do nothin' all the time.

June 5, 1858

Happy day in my life. I have found Daddy! He heard my whip-poor-will song when I was standing by the window. He whistled it right back. I looked down in the yard and there was a man.

First I did not know that it was Daddy standing there, though. His hair was white and his body was bony. He also had a long beard. But I hear that whip-poor-will song he makes and I know it has got to be Daddy.

June 6, 1858

I have my daddy again. He wrapped me in his strong arms. I tell him about the new baby who might have come already. I tell him that Mama is at Owl Creek with the Quaker people.

June 7, 1858

Roland and Corey Birdsong on the way to Owl Creek. Riding in a buggy. Roland still got his white hair and white beard. Only his hair is not truly white. He has put white powder on it. That way no one knows for true what he looks like. For me, I have a white cloth wrapped around my face like I got a toothache.

Mary Ellen and Dodd wrote us up some freedom papers. Not real freedom papers, but they will do if someone asks us for some.

June 8, 1858

The trip that took me many days is taking much shorter. That is because we are in a buggy and Daddy knows where he is going. He does not seem to be scared a bit that we will be stopped. We ride on the road right in the daylight. He say I must act like I got a toothache and put up a howl. So I howl and howl. Scare everyone away, even the catchers.

June 9, 1858

We stopped near a marsh. Was it that same marsh that I was lost in? I showed Daddy my book. He read it all through. He hugged me. I am so proud of you, son, Daddy say.

June 10, 1858

Daddy told me his story while we rode in the buggy. How he got cut by a slave catcher. How he got to Oberlin and saw posters about him everywhere. He went to a place called Sandusky. Canada is right across the lake from that place. Daddy worked for a man who has a big boat. Sometimes the man gives people like us rides over to the Canada side.

How come you didn't go to Canada yourself? I ask.

I couldn't do that, Daddy say. I must first have my family with me. He knew we were on the run. Just like Mama said, he had seen the poster about us. When he heard my whip-poor-will song, he had just then come back to Oberlin.

June 11, 1858

Strange thing. We stopped by the side of the road and walked into a swamp. Met a man there with his family. They are runaways. They been living in that swamp for nearly a year and nobody has found them yet.

Daddy and me saw a bird in that swamp, standing on one leg.

June 12, 1858

We are at Owl Creek. We see Mama. And I have a new baby sister! Mama is so happy. She didn't know we were coming. On the road not a soul stopped us. God's eye was on us. Daddy say now we will go to Sandusky. Then on to Canada. Freedom is almost here at last.

My baby sister is a sweet child. No name as yet. Mama say she wants me to be the one who names her.

June 13, 1858

We must hurry and leave. Word has come that Masser Hart is in nearby parts. Asking about us. He has not given up tracking us down. What he does not know is that the three of us are all together again. Also that the three of us are now four.

June 15, 1858
Sandusky, Ohio

Rode in back of a hay wagon. All of us covered with hay. Mama held the baby. She was quiet most of the time. Kind Quaker person drove us on the road. Drove night and day without sleep. Do not know his name. Just helped us because he felt like he wanted to. Happy to get out of that hay.

Later

We are at Second Baptist Church. Could
see the lake from the stairs. But soon as we got
here, we hid. I find a moment to record my
baby sister's name.

Star Birdsong.

I named her.

June 16, 1858
Lake Erie

How to find words to write what is in our
hearts.

We stand on the deck of the big boat. We
cross the ruff water. Land ahead!

Canada!

Sparrow crossing with us, too, fightin' the
wind.

I wear my red shirt.

Mama say you can't write out here on the deck, boy. The ink will waste. Daddy say let him try.

Roland, Angel, Star, and Corey Birdsong. We are free.

Underground Railroad be our freedom's wings.

Life in America
in 1857

Historical Note

By 1857, every state in the North had come out against slavery. But slave owners in the South were determined to hold onto their slaves. Since the arrival of the first slaves in 1620, African Americans had been struggling

Slaves work the fields on a plantation in the South.

Runaway slaves hide out in the swamps of Louisiana.

for their personal liberty. In 1857, two hundred and thirty-seven years later, that struggle was still going on.

From the earliest years of slavery, there are records of daring escapes. Men and women ran away, sometimes alone or with friends and family. They made their way through dense woods, fields, and swamps. They traveled in all kinds of weather, navigating by the stars at night and hiding out in caves

Runaways were angrily pursued by their owners.

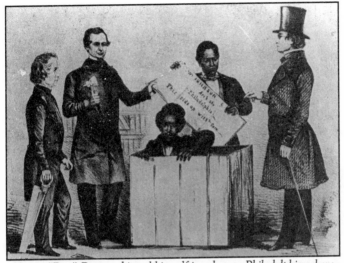

Henry "Box" Brown shipped himself in a box to Philadelphia where slavery had been outlawed.

or ditches during the day. Angry slave owners chased them with dogs and guns. The owners also posted advertisements asking for help in capturing the runaways. The posters described the fugitives and offered rewards.

The path to freedom was hard and frightening. The runaways sometimes got lost and had no food or water. Many were caught and forced back into slavery. But others got away. Those who made it were often helped out by a secret organization known as the Underground Railroad.

There were no trains on the Underground Railroad. The story goes that so many slaves escaped during the early 1800s that one slave owner made the remark that there must be "an underground railroad" running beneath the Ohio River, a known crossing point for fugitives. The Underground Railroad was a group of individuals who helped slaves on the journey to freedom. They were old and young, rich and poor, black, white, and Native American. Some belonged to religious groups such as the Quakers, Baptists, and Methodists. They called themselves "conductors" and hid escaping African Americans in "stations" along the way — barns, cellars, churches, and

300 DOLLARS

REWARD!

RUNAWAY from John S. Doak on the 21st inst., two **NEGRO MEN; LOGAN 45** years of age, bald-headed, one or more crooked fingers; **DAN 21** years old, six feet high. Both black. I will pay **ONE HUNDRED DOLLARS** for the apprehension and delivery of **LOGAN,** or to have him confined so that I can get him. I will also pay **TWO HUNDRED DOL-LARS** for the apprehension of **DAN,** or to have him confined so that I can get him.
JOHN S. DOAKE.
Springfield, Mo., April 24th, 1857.

This poster advertises a reward for the return of a slave to his owner.

tunnels. They gave the fugitives food, water, and forged freedom papers. They sometimes secretly transported them farther north in hay wagons, coaches, or boats. They helped them stow away in boxes and barrels — even in coffins! They left lamps burning in their windows at night to signal a safe hiding place.

The exact location of many stations on the Underground Railroad has remained a mystery to this day. The names of many of the

The Underground Railroad depended on the help of whites and free blacks to guide and protect runaways on their journey to freedom.

Harriet Tubman (far left) stands with slaves she helped free.

conductors also went unrecorded. We do know that free people of color such as Harriet Tubman and John Parker were part of the network. Both Tubman and Parker had escaped slavery themselves. Each of them made trips back to the South to lead runaways out. In the dark of the night, John Parker ferried people across the Ohio River. One well-known white conductor was Reverend

John Rankin, whose hilltop home in Ripley, Ohio, became a famous safe house. Added to these well-known heroes are hundreds of others whose names we will never know.

It was against the law to harbor escaping slaves. Underground Railroad conductors could be fined or put in jail if they were discovered. And under the Fugitive Slave Law of 1850, even if a slave did manage to cross over into a free state, such as Ohio, personal freedom was not guaranteed. If caught, a fugitive could be taken back to the South and forced into slavery again. This led many runaways to leave the United States altogether. For some, the final stop on the Underground Railroad was Canada.

The story of early African Americans and the Underground Railroad is a story of courage, conscience, and the ability to survive. It is the story of the struggle for personal liberty — an American story that belongs to us all.

About the Author

Sharon Dennis Wyeth is the author of *Once on This River*, named one of the 100 Titles for Reading and Sharing of 1998 by the New York Public Library; *Always My Dad*, a "Reading Rainbow Book"; and *Something Beautiful*, a Children's Book Council Notable Book in the field of Social Studies. She graduated from Harvard University.

"I recently learned the name of one of my ancestors, a free person of color. I wish I knew the story of how he got his freedom. I found it easy to slip into Corey's world. Part of that is because I've read so much history. But it's also because I feel close to my slave ancestors. Even though I don't know most of their names, I love them and admire them for their bravery. I also like nature. That's why I had Corey like birds. It gave me a chance to go birdwatching and to listen to birdsongs."

Sharon Dennis Wyeth lives with her family in Upper Montclair, New Jersey.

For Georgia

Acknowledgments

The author wishes to thank the following people and institutions for generously sharing their knowledge and publications with her: Betty Campbell of the John Parker Historical Society, Carl Westmoreland of the National Underground Railroad Freedom Center, Tom Appleton of the Kentucky Historical Society, Ohio naturalists Tom Thomson and Bob Conlon. Also to New Jersey Audubon Society, Schermann-Hoffman Sanctuary, and naturalist Mike Anderson for a lengthy consultation at the sanctuary. She also wishes to acknowledge her editor, Amy Griffin, whose skill and enthusiasm she greatly admires.

Grateful acknowledgment is made for permission to reprint the following:

Cover portrait and frontispiece by Glenn Harrington.

Page 95: Slaves work the fields on a plantation in the South, Library of Congress.

Page 96 (top): Runaways in the swamps of Louisiana, New York Public Library Picture Collection.

Page 96 (bottom): Pursuit of runaway, New York Public Library Picture Collection.

Page 97: Henry Brown, Brown Brothers, Sterling, PA.

Page 98: Reward poster, New York Public Library Picture Collection.

Page 99: "The Underground Railroad" by Charles T. Webber, #1927.26, Subscription Purchase Fund, Cincinnati Art Museum, Cincinnati, Ohio.

Page 100: Harriet Tubman, Sophia Smith Collection, Smith College, Massachusetts.

Other books in the My America series

Our Strange New Land
Elizabeth's Diary
by Patricia Hermes

The Starving Time
Elizabeth's Diary, Book Two
by Patricia Hermes

My Brother's Keeper
Virginia's Diary
by Mary Pope Osborne

Five Smooth Stones
Hope's Diary
by Kristiana Gregory

Westward to Home
Joshua's Diary
by Patricia Hermes

While the events described and some of the characters in this book
may be based on actual historical events and real people,
Corey Birdsong is a fictional character, created by the author,
and his diary is a work of fiction.

Library of Congress Cataloging-in-Publication Data
Wyeth, Sharon Dennis.
Freedom's Wings : Corey's diary / by Sharon Dennis Wyeth.
p.cm — (My America)
Summary: A nine-year-old slave keeps a diary of his journey to freedom along the
Underground Railroad in 1857.
0-439-14100-1
1. Underground railroad—Juvenile fiction. [1. Underground railroad—fiction. 2. Fugitive
slaves—Fiction. 3. Slavery—Fiction. 4. Afro-Americans—Fiction. 5. Diaries—Fiction.]
I. Title. II. Series.
PZ7.W9746 Fr 2001
[Fic]—dc21   00-059540
CIP AC

10 9 8 7 6 5 4 3 2 1   01 02 03 04 05

The display type was set in Quercus Hard.
The text type was set in Goudy.
Photo research by Zoe Moffitt
Book design by Elizabeth B. Parisi

Printed in the U.S.A. 23
First printing, May 2001